Motherhood Unplugged

Twisted tales of motherly spirit

Motherhood Unplugged

Twisted tales of motherly spirit

VISHALI THAKUR GARG

Anybook

Published By

Anybook

Cell : 9971698930

E-mail : contactanybook@gmail.com

Website : www.anybook.org

Price in India : 200/- INR

Paperback, First published by Anybook in 2022
Copyright © 2022 Anybook
Copyright Text © 2022 Vishali Thakur
Printed and bound in India
Cover Design & Typesetting by Anybook

ISBN : 978-93-91571-00-9

DEDICATED TO

I dedicate this book to Mumma & Papa...

About the Book

I chose to write on this subject as many fellow mothers are tired of traditional parenting myths and need a one-stop solution for all their parenthood questions, a like-minded partner in the beginning of their journey. This book will contain all the spheres of parenthood, covering from conception to raising the next generation. It will be an ode to all the mothers whose contribution is immense in the making of world-class citizens. We often forget to pat ourselves on our back as no one else gives us that credit for being a 24*7 mother, therefore, this book will remind mothers and fathers about their due share of understanding in so many twisted tales of vibrant parenthood, full of joys and tears.

The motive is to encourage people to think beyond what is said, what is heard, and what is right and make the choices for their heirs. We should not twist the sacred, and unconditional emotions behind the curtains of parenting challenges with mythological mindsets that restrict the opening passages of noble beliefs. This book will inspire and guide the parents and the upcoming generations looking for lesser rigorousness but the need of the hour is practical advice.

The core of my book is not educating people as I am not writing something new that they would not know, but we forgot ourselves amidst all the hustle and bustle. The central message revolves around not leaving yourself behind and not compromising on your dreams because kids are not a stumbling block but a building block of life around us. I want my readers to connect with their instincts as this is to make you feel relatable. If by any chance, I could revolutionise anyone's life to even a minor extent, my purpose of spreading the message would be fulfilled.

There are not dozens of bibliographies, but tons of emotions of different parents, grandparents, siblings, friends, and the societal outlook have been associated while co-relating with them. In the world of technological advancement and nuclear warfare, we are still stuck on the basics of life, and most of life goes about figuring out the right and wrong ways but not the happy ways of life.

The core happiness makes a patient healthy, not the medicines and procedural checkups. Likewise, parenting is a part of life but we forget to live to the fullest after becoming parents. This is a significant responsibility but not a hindrance that we halt our lives while raising our kids. We have entangled the threads of life that we are stuck in a circle of meaningless norms of society.

I am here to unplug the lives of people who are reading the book to relate to their journey when in doubt or overjoyed with wisdom. We must balance everything to create a happy environment of empathy, understanding and happiness.

This book is an ode to all the mothers and fathers and even those individuals who are the supporting system of this society, who help others grow, motivate and break the shackles of orthodoxy. I am grateful to all the mothers who have inspired me to write on this subject organically. All from the heart to relate with the readers of this modern generation. My heartfelt thanks to each individual who made me realise my capabilities to write and direct people at this younger age where I am still learning and life is an ongoing process of learning and un-learnings.

I am truly grateful to my Mentor, Gen Raj Mehta, as he has not only inspired but directed my point of views about life to be an all-rounder. His associations were not limited to military research, warfare, museums and art but life itself is a wonderful blend of everyday learning. His visionary teachings have inspired me to be more efficient towards everything I do in life.

About the Author

Vishali Thakur is a battlefield archaeologist, writer, explorer of the war zones, motivational speaker, team builder, wildlife enthusiast and photogtrapher. Majoring in Psychology, she is a Masters in Human Rights and a Diploma in Guidance and Counselling. Military research is her forte and she has contributed immensely as a Battlefield Archaeologist and Research Team Coordinator in the making of Punjab State War Heroes Memorial and Museum (PSWHMM), Amritsar. She has been a coordinator at several events, briefed the Chief Minister of Punjab, Western Army Commander and interacted with many war heroes and their families. She was a Senior Under Officer, NCC (Air Wing) Cadet and a 'C' Certificate holder. She served as Education Activist at Hamari Kaksha (NGO), Chandigarh. She has been a Face Painter at various Psychology Fests. Besides military research, writing about Motherhood is another area which interests her to simplify this eternal bond in the best way possible for all the generations to come.

Content

Dividing the Borders...
Motherhood or Parenthood?

I always wonder why it is called 'motherhood' and not 'parenthood' when the idea of being a parent generate in the minds of two. In our societal norms, it's pretty easy to divide the lines of everything and for that matter, we do not even leave the concept of baby-making to baby raising.

A journey from confusion to conception, for all the mothers dealing with their limitations in their ways-ends-means, a fascinating moment of crossing your fingers to see those two red lines of joyful hope and happiness, no matter what is going in life, amidst all the chaos and demons of debates associated with right age, right time and so on... a woman knows the worth of having that tiny tot to complete her life.

Adopting happiness...? Well, that's another fantastic way to feel the warmth of this everlasting bond as we inherit the roots of such unconditional love from Yashoda and little Krishna. Do we need to divide this unconditional love of the parents? Parenthood is a journey that faces differentiated ups and downs, a journey to create an eternal bond with mind and soul, an organic relationship where you learn and un-learn with each passing day to re-discover our own potentialities.

Mothers have a particular case that needs no comparison but an understanding of being the originator of life in this universe...our mother earth, she is also an originator of so many micro and macro living beings and likewise women are blessed with this divine power of fertility to nourish lives. To sustain generations, the ultimate onus is on a woman as that's the power of the womb when a woman steps into a selfless journey of motherhood. She wears a unique but vastly responsible crown of expectations with a graceful smile and hope.

Hope is a unique feature where we re-build and re-gain our strength each time in life's journey, not only in parenting but overall touching different facets of daily challenges of joy and stress.

These divisions of parenting are human-induced in this world at large. These were never pre-determined naturally. We, humans, are mainly influenced by external factors than following our God-gifted instincts. Instinct is a distinctive attribute that is innate and specially available to make us wiser and more logical to follow what is right and break certain stereotypes.

A stereotypical mindset is a choice we make, it is not mandatory to lead a complex life and the thinking associated with specific subjects of concern like parenting, societal norms, myths, superstitions and so on...

We talk about the progress of science and the technologies in the fields of Artificial Intelligence and how science has eased the entire process of having kids without defining the criteria. That's science but we are the originators of that facility as we can use it the way we want to but why don't we direct our super minds guided by instincts to differentiate between what is logical and illogical.

In the following procedures, we tend to forget humanity. Little joys of being empathetic towards society as we become the stumbling blocks in the way of our creative outlook and most importantly we have become slaves of our age-old set norms which needs to be modified with time.

The demand of time is always different and it can never be stagnant. We spend most of our time in the calculations of rules of parenting than actually trying to know the realm of what makes it more special...laws, superstition or total freedom for all the human beings to choose their coarse of parenting style.

We must become empathetic and responsible towards each other to ease the definition of actual parenthood so that people should embrace this eternal bond of lifetime happiness. This unconditional, undefined happiness has different meanings across parents and gender.

Gender...a very artificial distinctive feature inbuilt

into our memory system. We do not want to break the shackles of double thinking as we contradict the standards of humans as per our thoughts, situations and what appeals to us to hear, see, talk about and get comfortable with.

While setting the norms, we forget to become just human, a human-like, not so jinxed and judgmental about others' choices...a little blend of understanding while passing through different phases of life is sufficient to justify our role play in this world.

We get too hard on ourselves and sometimes for others as well. That line of balance between what is right and wrong, coming and going, losing and gaining, needs the art of constructive assessment to set a stage for so many hopes around us, be it our friends, family, kids, men, women, animals and each creature on this planet who wants to breathe the way they want to while defining their own relaxations and limitations of life as per their circumstances.

Be that pleasant air for others because what we give, we receive in return. You will also gradually get that warmth from people around you which will engulf your mind with positivity and an appreciating nature to embrace others as they are with a lot of ease.

What we can leave behind is the choice we made consciously. We do not lack wisdom but hold back ourselves to acquire that courage to be a part of that change holistically.

Our development is when we spill the beans of understanding and empathy for others. We should be interactive in learning the different dimensions of life. Only then we will be able to pass this on to our generations a thread of unconditioned and non-judgemental love and affection. They will be the face of our upbringing and the direction to the dreams of aspirations we have engraved in their outlook. Leave the legacy of your unsaid contribution as a trademark of a privileged human who came into this world to revolutionise the societal norms for the betterment of humans rather creating a vicious circle of negativity and judgemental societal parameters defining ideal parents. Nothing is perfect and ideal as change is the constant law of nature.

The Trimester Truffle

Truffle is a perfect name for a ball of chocolate ganache dusted with cocoa. Likewise, the journey is a beautiful rollercoaster ride of many evolving emotions inside the womb. That tiny being becomes a part of knowing yourself much deeper despite a lot of self-talk...a questioning mind all day long.

Someday you will get up filled with tons of energy and some other day you will be high on mood swings right from getting up from the bed. That is how a mother also grow along with her baby when she becomes a cute truffle of stubbornness, seeking validation, throwing tantrums, and needing someone to meet her demands of crazy cravings and an endless affectionate gesture of nothing but unconditional understanding.

The journey of motherhood passes through various stages from day one to the delivery room. Two lives work together to make that miracle happen along with family and friends support. For a woman, it is always a unique and inexplicable feeling of how I would manage this or that. She breaks the barriers of fear and tries to get into that zone of being someone who learns to control anger issues and develop a lot of patience while carrying the baby, keeping all the meticulous details protecting the baby in her womb from eating right to sleeping on her left. A baby becomes a guiding armour for a mum. She becomes a hero for her baby in the way she protects him/her in the womb and then from all the evil eyes throughout her life as she lives for her pieces of heart.

An efficient mother goes through a series of emotions before becoming a wise momma...the emotions make her aware of the child when she sees her little heart out of her own body. A mother becomes an encyclopaedia of knowing even the minutest things about her child.

Trimester by trimester, she becomes an enlightened one to guide others along helping people to relate to similar events of parenthood, breaking their myths and fears...she transforms her identity adding many stars of wisdom through her experiences.

Each trimester unfurls the stages of motherhood; a careless woman to a respond would be mum! Each passing day either starts with the bowls of anxiety, rushing hours to the washroom or puking now and then. The body works 24*7 to produce a life inside the holy womb, from a tiny zygote to a bloomed bundle of joy... Kicks and cramps become the new regular part of life.

Isn't it a God's miracle that how this beautiful Goddess of fertility and a life-generating superwoman

passes through all the phases so graciously... Mothers are special, indeed...

The preparation of the arrival... A checklist tickles constantly in her mind welcoming her new self in the maternity gown. It is linked with many questions coming to a mother's mind before stepping into the actual position of being a momma. The sense of pain can never make you mentally prepared with the painful tales you hear from others' experiences until or unless you get into that D-Day.

There are many rituals for welcoming the little pie and a fight back spirit to the postpartum depression, checking the feeds every other hour, burping the baby for hours and evolving a new sleeping habit; sleep wherever you sit.

Was it a normal delivery or a c-section? This question stresses a new mother who starts wondering if she is some lesser than the normal birth-giving mums, battling with her new life, feeding the baby amidst that immense pain where one hand is occupied with the oximeter and the other with cannula followed by non-stop bleeding... there comes that divine super powerful motherly strength which embraces all the pain and depression in that joyful moment.

Postpartum depression is an underrated subject of discussion as we are much more ignorant about the things that must be addressed with utmost care and concern. This depression varies from woman to woman. Some get through it quickly whereas some take time. Are we ready to give a new mum her sweet time to get

					Motherhood Unplugged

over that period? Do we care about her mental health post delivery? We all ignore and the mother also avoids and carries forward without admitting it.

The hormonal system goes under stress and we don't consider the grave need to normalise it. Many women do not know about it as we never spread the word. Many knows regarding this but ignore thinking it is a part of motherhood, well, yes, it is, but...we should normalise it, talk about it, do something about it, speak your heart out, if you feel like crying unnecessarily then cry your lungs out but do not hide your emotions.

We often forget to look after our mental health, which goes through a massive transition of responsibilities and new challenges ahead of unknown parents. Postpartum depression in a mum and stress levels in a father is different as both of them go through many phases of parenthood from pre-conception to the labour room...a matter of so many emotions revolving around head and heart.

Another area of the most discussed subject is weight gain...which we all discuss and debate. Sometimes we end up body-shaming ourselves as well. Every woman and her post-delivery routine is different. Some are working, some live alone, some have family support and some hires a full-time nanny.

With back-to-back feeding sessions, no sleeping routine, a disturbed hormonal imbalance, a messed-up home and some parents do babysitting in shifts to get some sleep in bits and pieces because having a sound sleep becomes something too much to wish for. Amidst all the hustle and bustle how are we supposed to look like Kate Middleton...spick and span, addressing the media outside the Lindo Wing having a perfect physique even after delivering three kids...much appreciated but we all are different genetically and physically as well. Take it easy on yourself and take as much time as you want to return to your yoga/gym/long walks routine. Our lives, challenges and circumstances to raise a baby to run a house can never match with one another. Accepting the dissimilarities is another area of learning.

Having good health is essential, and weight management goes hand-in-hand. Start with simple exercises and be patient with your body and the results. Do not stress over stretch marks, hair fall, itchy skin etc. Deal with it one by one, consult a dietician if you want to or do your own research to get back into your previous self.

Do take your time but start looking after yourself as well. Being a mum doesn't mean you can't look after yourself. You must rejuvenate your body-soul-mind because a healthy mum is what a home needs...

Take charge of your body gradually and do not get stuck in the name of motherhood that I do not have time, I can't manage to look after myself. Women are super women who look after the entire home but cannot spare time for themselves. Is it fair on your part? An all-rounder woman can do anything and can do wonders if she will look after her body and mind.

There you're, lady...re-define and transform yourself...no one can stop you but your own self.

A Labelled Mother

Labelling human emotions...we often go with the flow without realising the repercussions which would affect our lives and the surroundings in which we co-exist. Humans do not learn the art of co-existence as we are social animals, and our actions and reactions depend on how we think...like-minded is impossible each time. Still, constructive thoughts, solutions, empathy, and unconditional understanding pave an excellent way for us to evolve many folds of human potential.

A choice of being a mother, not being a mother, surrogacy, single parenting, and separation of parents should be a personal choice of people around us, be it our friends or family or our children. We impose on others and on ourselves as well the fabricated relations in the name of parenthood but parenting blesses the humans; it does not trap any of us...we put those shackles in the way of our life. We start labelling everything even if others don't.

Motherhood Unplugged

Labels of responsibilities, expectations, do's and don't's, perfect parents to not so perfect parents...

We exaggerate the limits of being too demanding about the least important things rather than exercising the strong will of the human mind which talks about sense and logic and gives us the freedom to be what we want. If we did not accept our choices, we would not be firm on our beliefs then how can we assume that our kids should be more precise in their perspectives about life, career, and relationships...?

The need of the hour is the seeds of revolutionary, upfront, logical wisdom wrapped with empathy. We are divided in our minds which we sometimes confuse too much. This too much has become a new normal these days despite much scientific progress, we do not skip to shame, or if we would not, we will surely make our point despite its need. Do not discourage if you cannot encourage people about their own choices. Right to Life (Article 21) of our Indian Constitutions has widened the scope of personal preferences and liberties as we update ourselves as per changing times and demands generations to generations. We lack and differ when it comes to revolutionising little thoughts one-by-one. Charity begins at home, but we want to change the world first.

Embracing a change, whether we like it or disagree with it has nothing to do with interfering and dragging down the tiny steps which have always been taken in the progress of humanity. We become our own enemies while justifying societal norms. Norms are from humans

    Motherhood Unplugged

to discipline them, to give them a direct in need but we shrink the scope of revising the norms. Why can't we rise above these narrow ways of labelling emotions? It isn't that impossible to achieve because starting from where we are would surely make a way through tricky but staying stagnant won't lead us anywhere. Make a beautiful way of hope for others who think differently, want to be different, and don't want to show a leisurely passage of life.

Motherhood is a blessing not a tagline to tag your responsibilities. Can you ever wonder how a single father can be a mum to his kids? Can we ever think out-of-the-box that a gay or a lesbian couple or a transgender person can also dare to share the same twisted tales where they are not being judged but rather feel encouraged? We need that comforting environment in our society to raise a world-class generation. We have introduced new categories of male/female/homosexual/LGBTQ but never implemented them in their entirety. A uterus doesn't make a mother mum, but acknowledging this beautiful feeling makes a person a mother or a motherly father. Surrogacy has paved the way for each of us where the age and gender of a person is no bar.

Empathising and encouraging the fellow mothers to introduce a new ray of humanity which is the actual need of the hour as we hear horrifying news of rapes, dowry and disgrace to women worldwide.

Raising a life is a responsibility, not fanaticism, unquote the same world with unlike mindsets in the same society. It is an idea of transforming the outlook of humanity to be kind, fair and just for the upbringing of India class citizens, representing the idea of equality and humanism instead beating the same drum of orthodox beliefs.

Beliefs are what we start believing as individuals and pass on to others, therefore, being judgemental is the easiest thing a person can do, but being empathetic and giving space to others to bloom outside their limitations is an actual act of humanity. Accepting people around us the way they are would break the labeled taboos of our society.

We need to detox the seeds of hypocritical thinking to accept the new normal of society. We as humans look at each case with a little mind, and start labelling each person to fit them in a box of labels in our subconscious mind. Humans have the intellect to disintegrate what is right and wrong, therefore, in the calculations of right and wrong, we forget to grow ourselves to break the chain of a prejudiced outlook.

The change I am talking about is a collective responsibility as a compassionate society owes to this nation where we accept everyone with graciousness and an open mind. A humble graceful heart is all what the world needs. An open mind equipped for a constructive change for the society is still a dream. We are least bothered about these changes when renowned celebrities break the chains of stereotypes but are not tolerant when it comes to normal individuals in our surroundings.

Likewise, if a mother or father is a divorcee, society

looks at their kids with different opinions and is always ready to pass on negative judgments. Not only in their childhood but throughout their lives, they have to bear the cost of such choices, which are not explicitly made by their parents joyfully but only due to unavoidable circumstances to give a peaceful life to their kids because in a negative environment no one can co-exist happily.

Is it too much to ask for not being judgemental and letting everyone live per their wish...? Do we ever try to pass on the positive wavelength of genuine understanding towards each other? Doing so will pass on a legacy of humanity, compassion, tolerance, and empathy for others in our young generation. We build each other, isn't it?

We seek a better environment for our children but forget to ease the environment and their surroundings with a positive outlook towards people living with us. We do not perform our collective responsibility but rather try to deviate our ways from the adversaries and hard truths of some other people and their kids that they are going through. We need to play our part for a gradual reform we intend to see in the action of others.

The path of the overall development of one's child is different for each of us. Still, collectively we all belong to the ordinary mindset of constructive upbringing from toddler to adolescent age and beyond. Psychologically speaking, the external environment plays a vital role in the overall development of one's personality. What we learn at home makes us more stronger to deal with the different challenges of day-to-day life accordingly outside our comfort zone. Likewise, when we come back home, we bring back the wisdom from those challenges, which creates a way for sculpting our personality traits.

Wise life choices for our kids make the parenting style different for redefining the boundaries of cognitive development and creating a valuable asset for the society as we belong to a rich culture, which is a blend of unity in diversity.

Depression
Relatives
ADVISES
No space

I vs They : Relative-stigma

From delivering a baby to raising a child and fighting postpartum depression, a mother gradually evolves a let-go syndrome. Mental sanity and happiness need to defeat the odds of this motherly journey. Hence, a mum can do anything! The relatives play a significant role in guiding and supporting, but age-old myths engulf their minds to such an extent that they do pass on from generation to generation.

Mental Health...a most under-rated subject of grave concern to deal effectively with postpartum depression as it can sometimes take several months to years if not dealt with properly. A self-care regimen goes out of the window as everybody around the new mum is more bothered about the baby in terms of don't eat this, its not good for the baby, don't do this, its harmful for the baby, but nobody understands that a woman needs equal utmost care after delivering the baby as the body has already gone through a lot of physical wear and tear along with that a significant responsibility of a child and dealing mentally/physically with the new surroundings takes time. An unconditional support from her partner, understanding, supportive, positive vibes, encouragement and appreciation for breastfeeding her child despite her own aches and wounds. A new beginning has begun for each of us, and she is also a part of that process. We start making her understand as if she is conditioned already. Parenting is a gradual process, it is a never ending of emotions, care, love, and respect. The advises she receives when everyone rewinds the process of when we became mums we did this, we did that etc etc but everybody tells you all the good parts of it, but no one makes her understand certain hardships that a mum has to go through that she can be a little difficult at times while going through a lot stress already...isn't it? We have made everything way too procedural that the scientific advancements, myth-breaking paths for the ease of parenthood with the help of many things like breast pumps, sterilisers and cloth diapering are still a thing to wonder about in many cases. We don't participate to be a part of the solution rather complicate and becomes another problem that hugely confuses a young mum that she starts doubting her God-gifted motherly instincts.

Instincts become another new normal in parenting, guiding all the phases of parenthood. Self-doubts become a hurdle when we do not associate with like-minded vibe from our comfort zones whom we call our friends and family. When a baby is born, many other relations are born along...mum, papa, grandparents, aunts and uncles. We all get promoted and the promotion brings responsibilities, too, and these responsibilities are mutual to make lives better, happy and blissful rather than more depressing, challenging, and demanding.

It is a stigma of not being rational but emotional, this is not the generation but the generations gap. It becomes tremendously tricky for a new mum whether to listen to the paediatricians, google or simply rely on her motherly instinct.

Things get complicated and one feels trapped in the vicious circle of saying yes or no. Why can't we break the taboo of formalities as women should understand that sensitive heart with empathy and like-mindedness provide space to learn and unlearn motherhood's twisted tales?

The solitary practices are a must for a new mum to explore the dimensions of motherhood. What suits her best, sleep timings, things to do while managing a new addition in her routine, social aspects and more than these, a date with her new version as a mum...

The elders of the family generally pressure a mum to have ample rest and sleep to the maximum...but this helps a woman ease and heal her physical aches and wounds. Still, some women do want to get social, talk to their friends, learn about their testimonies of parenthood, relating it to their journey as this comforts a new mum in the initial days of post pregnancy. In these times, and that's the best therapy to get out of that zone of postpartum depression is to call or video call a friend, family member or whosoever is in your list of favourites because when we talk we exhale that underlying stress.

A woman, a mum, a wife, a daughter and so on... enveloped in so many relations, seeks that 'Me Time' space...and that space should be everlasting as raising a baby from infancy to the different milestones needs extraordinary courage where she becomes a certified multitasking Mom-zilla to do things accordingly... Sometimes it's five minutes before or after; how does that matter as long as she is given her space to understand the nitty-gritty of life as a whole.

If we discuss the concept of space, then it may sound selfish for some and much needed for some as every individual has some way or the other different perception about having their own space. Space doesn't mean running away from the responsibilities, and it should also not be a matter of guilt to have your own space and time whenever the need arises. We confuse and intermix the whole circumstance with unnecessary assumptions. At times, a mum must sit and relax, take a back seat, and come back fully charged to the baby positively and energetically. It's called dividing the responsibilities, and sometimes it's okay to leave specific tasks which you think are not that important for that moment. You can breathe for a while, inhale the positivity out of that monotonous routine, exhale the tiredness and re-build yourself each time of the day.

It's essential to break the barriers of monotony, as the entire life becomes a full circle of the same routine

Motherhood Unplugged

for a couple of years. One needs to evolve in such an environment not only for themselves but for the positive upbringing of the child as well. This break is not only mother centric but for all the family members involved in the process of raising the baby as it is a collective responsibility. We must extend our shoulders to each other to vent our emotions freely.

This understanding makes a mother's job relatively easy and less hectic when we know we can detox our minds from negative thoughts, burdens and stress of daily hassles. We have a few people to talk to who always extend their hands in need and are ready to empathise in the best and worst times, as motherhood is an endless journey.

Having a full-time nanny for the baby is another aspect of giving the same treatment to someone there to help you in your parenthood where you are handing over your trust with a piece of your heart. This is something appreciable as parents resume their work life because someone is there to look after the baby. Day care centres and personal nannies has widened the scope of becoming parents and pursuing the dreams of their lives as well.

Ensuring great respect for such individuals is a must as its their job, they are getting paid for it but humanity opens the gates of a happy environment where the baby has to be raised. By doing so, we ensure an employment generation in the society and encourage more people who are keen on looking after the baby as one of their noble professions. That's how we extend a helping hand to each other.

Whether it's relatives who are a support system in your life, friends, or a nanny, the respect should always be unbiased and unconditional because these are the steps that are the building stones of a balanced upbringing of your child. The child start learning right from the womb, therefore, we should always be careful about our behaviour with others and even with our own self as well. We can never be perfect all the time in every situation but little by little we learn while raising that tiny piece of our heart.

Life around two B's Breastfeed, Burp-Repeat

Monotony, boredom, stagnant, stuck, and the list of synonyms goes on and on when it comes to raising a little life entirely dependent upon ourselves. A baby understands when they are a tiny being in the womb, therefore, we always advise mothers to stay happy, spiritual, and eat healthy principle becomes a new addition to the list.

Our actions and reactions get transferred in terms of energies to our baby even when he/she is just a day older or a year older or becomes an adult. Amidst this monotony, we vent our emotions, frustrations and complaints...we freak out in short.

It is common and easy to understand as mother is a human too. She gets confined in the monotony of the life cycle that at times that she forgets herself and her own existence gets fit into bits and pieces, those intervals simultaneously take a toll upon her mental and physical health. It becomes more challenging when people call her a mum next to Goddess, and then the scam begins...a scam of fair and unfair hopes, demands and always on her toes, a never tiring woman who wraps herself from one responsibility to another to another. As she grows her roles and responsibilities also increases. A life cycle of a woman always hover around choices...she has to drop one choice to make another.

We are also humans, accept it. We, women, create an imaginary world of extremism...extreme affection, extreme worries, and extreme fears of all kinds make her life more challenging to handle. She must understand that she is a mother to her child, not a nanny who can't complain, who can't express what it sometimes means to miss her old self, old life, and those me-time flashbacks when she sits with herself.

We live a very fabricated life which starts and ends with tons of expectations from a mother who is responsible for everything and she cannot even complain about anything because if she does, she is not a good mum as each mum has to go through the same phase so why this crib...? Expression of emotions makes half a life easier for her and others as they can know the actual cause of annoyance rather assuming and blaming her for having mood swings. She gets misunderstood with the lack of expressions and gets a tag of oh yeah, she is always complaining, hurt, constantly annoyed and people choose to ignore her emotional needs. Be firm to make your point crystal clear, speak when needed, and do not let others assume on the basis of temporary mood swings as that's the image they will carry forward about you before others and the vicious circle of blame games never really end. Make a way for yourself on your own and never let others take charge of your emotions, what are you supposed to feel and say...say it as we believe in democracy at large, and it begins at home first. Make yourself responsible enough and own what you think like it's a great way to express our real self and expectations to admit, deny, apologise, or ask for an apology. These are the precious stepping stone you will pass on to your children as their learning curve in life as kids do what they see us doing, and staying firm on our principles is a remarkable upbringing as parents one can pass on to... Now, let me come back to the point of burping the baby...

Have we ever wondered about the eternal struggle to burp the baby right...? It is much more than what it sounds...as colic babies are the most difficult to ease for the parents who do not know what's happening to the apple of their eyes. The repeat cycle is a task force for a mum followed by other family members of the family...

Advises, reading, and doing almost a Ph.D. on burp, colic, and tummy roll. What not...there comes another addition, tummy time to the baby, and then again, a mum wonders how much time is it safe, texting fellow mothers, hurriedly making the asafoetida paste leads her to a mixed emotional state of mind.

The struggle doesn't end as it keeps taking the form of one another each day and time. Amidst all the facilities, products, doc on a call availability...a mum is a mum. The emotional unease is constant in the initial journey. For her, it's nothing less than a pandemic as the world goes upside down when a baby cries inconsolably. Meanwhile, she will hear that you may be not eating the right food, having a lot of spices, oily, or heavy stuff which makes

                    Motherhood Unplugged

your baby uneasy, leading to gas problems.

Here comes a situation when a mum starts doubting each action and frames a self-critic image of herself... I am not supposed to eat pickles, fritters, or spicy food and end up making it even worse while being too hard on herself.

Easy!!! It's my piece of advice, momma... There can always be a mid-way in every situation as you can't stay in a self-guilt zone ruining your peace of mind over petty issues. The main problem is that babies understand emotionally even if they can't speak or express themselves. The frowning forehead, a worrisome environment is not needed around that sweet little life. It would be best if you are little careful about your emotional well-being as the only person who can understand what a mum is going through is her own-self.

Why do you seek validations for all your actions? Balance is the key to everything as over-eating is not suitable for mum, likewise, overfeeding is not good for the baby because we all have one solution to fix the baby's cry is...feed the baby. They must be hungry or need to be relaxed, so just feed, and that will fix it all together, but it cannot be the case every time. Sometimes the babies expresses themselves by simply crying as that is the only language all the babies have to express themselves. We want to fix everything in the quickest possible way and do not want the baby to cry most of the time...is that fair to the baby?

We all follow the impractical ways to temporarily curb the situation temporarily as who will see the long-term consequences in such a hurry. Trust me, sometimes handling the baby with ease is another art of parenting that teaches immense patience and reacting with lesser irritation at things that are not as problematic as we perceive is a life changing quality which transforms us from average to better version of our own-selves. Look for creative methods to deviate the child, don't feed the baby unnecessarily when you know that the baby is well fed.

Spend time, and create a bond with the baby beyond feeding sessions also. Try to make it simple, think like a child making it easier to get through that situation. We worry more and react immediately. We must ensure and inculcate a habit of understanding the law of nature that the babies get settle down accordingly as our kids want us to be as simple as they are, innocent, going with the flow and take it easy.

We complicate it with our concern and overthinking, and first-time parents undoubtedly get worried. It's natural, but we should also accept this process of the baby's physical development naturally because that takes time to adjust from the mother's feed to formula, formula milk to semi-solids followed by coming entirely on the family food...this a gradual process where a journey from a tiny baby to a full-grown toddler is a remarkable sign of growth. Likes/dislikes evolve, tantrums for food, bedtime routine, and the list goes on and on...

Take it the way it is, as over-stressing yourself will not change the law of nature, and the entire process will take its time. Take your own time to understand the unavoidable facts about parenthood, accept them, try to be calm and follow it peacefully. It simplifies your parenthood journey, and you enjoy the process rather cribbing. In the end, it's all about how we handle and pass on this to one another as for working parents and single parents, it becomes a nightmare after such a hectic schedule to settle the cycle of their lives according to the baby's routine. People with family support get over this phase with their help. Embracing the phases of parenthood with some tactics make it more convenient and lesser hectic physically and mentally.

Godzilla or Momzilla-Pee/Poop or Party

A mother is never off duty just like a soldier... always protective, our guiding armour, torch bearer, and a go-to-person in every situation. From a woman to she becomes a multitasking Godzilla...That is a transformation a woman gets ahead with and starts a journey in which she sees her life in the flashbacks of nostalgia. She misses her carefree life but joyfully enters into the new era never-ending responsibilities because the trimesters end superficially but the new phases of her child's milestones makes her get along as far as she can to ensure all the possibilities of a happy upbringing.

A legacy of a mother who stays with her children life-long in terms of daily drill of discipline to moral values which they follow and the chain goes on...we need to differentiate between what we want to leave behind as an imprint of our never fading legacy.

A mother is not only a mother but an individual as well, an individual who is not a nanny to her child instead, it's an emotional blend of so many things which revolve around her life. She keeps relating to her parenting style, mends her ways accordingly, and sometimes gets along with her instinct. The transformation continues throughout her life, meeting different life challenges of balancing parenting, life, home and professional life. Then, she comes to her turn if she ever gets any time out of that busiest life cycle.

Her drills are fixed from the moment she gets up to make her kids sleep. She never complains about the monotonous routine she has to follow whether she wants it, likes it, or doesn't like it at times. She adjusts everything in the name of an affectionate bond with her kids. Even if she is not well, she won't take a break but always on her toes...mum life, you see! An unconditional, unspoken bond for which she doesn't get any standard operating procedure, that's God gifted, and ,therefore, mothers are special...an abode of immense love and care that she forgets herself to remember the life of her kids, their routine, discipline, food, poo, pee, doctors, vaccination and the list adds on. She becomes an all-rounder go-to-mum naturally, but we make her life a little tricky with unsolicited expectations that are not needed. The calculations are pretty straightforward when it comes to a woman...she only expects 'understand me' sort of support as she is capable of handling the entire world around her; all she needs is a parallel companionship where she doesn't feel that I am a loner sometimes in this journey of life. A shoulder to rely upon when she gets through the ups and downs of parenthood.

There are many ironies of life, but the combination of pee/poop getting along with a party is a universal drill; on-the-toes... Can a woman think of this extraordinary multitasking talent and mental calculations like micro-managing every minute of her life revolving around that little happiness and how her entire schedule adjusts accordingly every day as each day is a surprise. Be it her office, social life, personal life, or even it's about love-making...

We don't talk about women's mental health and they also tend to ignore it in the name of additional responsibilities of motherhood. Women never really unwind their minds from heart. A day out, a phone call, a conversation full of complaints to her spouse, honest confessions which hover around her head and heart as that works as a detox of so many unsaid, unfelt emotional wear and tear...its should be an integral part of everybody's life be it man or woman. Emotional breaks is the word!

We carry forward that annoyance, irritation, and monotony of typical mindset and behaviour of either being too tired or my life is stuck for a couple of years. Mothers are also human, I repeat. We take ourselves for granted and realise losing a significant part of our identity when it's too late.

Where does our hobbies figure out in that busiest daily schedule? Do we ever question or introspect to know the needs of our conscience? We simply state...where's the time? Time will never come and we have to snatch a few moments of mental sanity, emotional detox and ample space to unwind to cleanse the stressful cache.

It is also a part of parenting, a significant step to giving something to our offspring as an art of living, a sophisticated way to pass on such legacies important for their well-being and society.

Never stop a heart that wants to bloom in the gloomy days of demotivation and negative thoughts, and when you feel this is it, there is no way to move further to break the shield of helplessness. When the tussle between heart and head goes beyond to re-assure and affirm that I can manage, I can do, and I can dare to achieve and dream despite all odds and stones in my way.

The coarse of life is full of ups and downs where we fall many times and get up, we feel failed as parents, sometimes as an individual when we are unable to meet the work and household responsibilities the way we assume to meet our targets and that overburden us. It's okay to lag behind when you're mentally and physical ly exhausted as the right state of mind is much needed to deal with those gloomy days.

We all think like parents and forget to feel like a human who needs refreshments, short breaks and some days to fully rejuvenate our mind from the daily hassles of life. We always try to become a perfect example but this world is not perfect. All we need to do is to unfurl the world around us slowly. We get too harsh on ourselves which we pass on to our kids. A frustrating moment in which you yell at kids, sometimes unnecessarily scolding them and feeling wrong about that... goes on and on even after self-pledges and promises that I will not do it next time.

This complex procedure is an age old method the way our parents dealt with their surroundings but the present time is full of external pressure on parents and kids as well where they barely enjoy their childhood. We all need to learn the art of going easy with each other, it's a supreme art of easy parenting, which requires a lot of patience and emotional stability. The tussle between parents is also another cause of concern that kids feel neglected at home.

Therefore, parents need to pursue what they like as that works as a therapy for the mind when we meet new people, talk to them, and get some time for ourselves that kind of break is enough from that monotonous routine. When we bring joy at home, the environment becomes pleasant for all of us. We should not ignore developing some skills, learning something online if time is the issue, and transforming ourselves from time to time with time is a great way to deal with the toxicity and unwanted stress levels. These little efforts in the right direction make a massive difference in our lives.

We hesitate to ourselves that we barely have any idea about our skills, strengths, weaknesses, etc. This type of behaviour leads to so much confusion as we lack making the right decisions at times, therefore, it is a chain which starts from one end of confusion to another as we keep on building our lifestyle along with this chain and confined our creative thinking around it. We do not

Motherhood Unplugged

try to think beyond and push ourselves out of our comfort zone of procrastinations. Do not get stuck anywhere in life in the name of parenting and responsibilities. It's a part of our life but you also exist there in your life where we all forget to acknowledge our super abilities.

Each parent has different challenges that's why it is necessary to look at your life exclusively in terms of your strengths and what you expect from your life. Make a choice, take a decision, and do not stop yourself from achieving it, at least try your level best without getting worried about the results. We compare, and that comparison also becomes a stumbling block, therefore, it is always advisable not to see what others are doing and how they are managing but carve your own way to reach where you want to. Be different and become an example to motivate fellow parents around you with your actions, not your words.

Motherhood Unplugged

A Confused Momma : Salt or no salt, sugar or no sugar

Life is a mixture of a sweet and salty journey, isn't it? Mothers complicate it when they start dissolving that mixture in their kid's life. Food becomes a magical experience or an absolute mess for a mum and her child. Introducing taste to our children defines their eating habits as we either convert them into picky eaters or force feed followed by neglecting their yes/no signal when the child tries to convey it in their own way.

There comes another debate: are we supposed to give salt or sugar in the first year? This debate gets on the nerves of a mum to such an extent that it leads to confusion and a tussle between right and wrong gets dragged endlessly. We neglect the basics of food, making it a complex process even for others around us.

The threads of self-doubt, endless readings on the internet, seeking advice, and not fixing your heart at your instinct make this experience gloomy and irritating. What should be an ideal diet for my child? We decide not as per a child's requirement or capacity but force-feeding, feeding with distractions, and going to such an extent which satisfies a mother's soul. While satisfying herself, she forgets the basics of human anatomy...do we eat when we don't feel like it? Is that overfeeding makes a baby healthier? Can we eat when we are inconsolably crying due to that vaccination pain or fever or whatever could be the reason? You gave birth to a human, so how can your child function differently? We neither provide a break nor understand the grass-root level habits which form the basis of a child's happy eating and healthy eating habits. We beat around the bush and exhaust the beautiful process of eating joyfully. We look out for solutions but the necessity is to look within, questioning our doubts, and try to resolve the state of confusion because that is what we pass on to our precious kids. We are here to imbibe a simplified life but complicate it without rectifying the actual cause of worry. We get worried, scared, and assume so much, which distorts the process of being in the present moment. As we say, eating is essential, but happy eating creates a massive difference in the child. Happy kids rejuvenate the environment naturally, and a cranky climate is not suitable for anyone, be it parents or kids.

Confusions are a mother's best friend. A million-dollar question salt or no salt, doctor's advice, friend's concern or in-law's guidance or the baby's taste and tantrums...? What should my heart follow? We tend to become over-protective, over-thinker, and over-analyse in life. Minute things concern us even the slightest change scares us sometimes, and we over-burden our mind unnecessarily.

My friend follows this routine, the doctor advises something else, and so on. First of all, do what your heart think is right. God gifted intuitions are the real power of women so why do we doubt ourselves? Just because we are mothers, we need to have a reasoning for everything like Einstein? Aren't we enough to raise the baby as per our choices and the resources available?

The preferences and life choices differ in each house for every mother. We must stop looking out and look inside that motherly heart of gold. We deviate from the basic concept of introducing homely food and taste to the baby and start wondering about irrelevant things.

More than salt and sugar, we get stuck at 'are we doing right?' Mothers must acquire that confidence from themselves alone. No one will do the needful for you...follow your heart and wit, that's all.

Salt and sugar composition for your child doesn't define your caliber as a mother, instead, your positive outlook makes you stand different from the crowd. We, as mother, are not a logbook to maintain such details rather we need to see our actual growth of patience in introducing the food and taste to the child in a natural way without harassing your mind and as per child's appetite, likes/dislikes, and why don't they like certain foods as what you need to develop in your child is healthy eating habits, what should be the time gap in between the meals and snacks, what are the different options to offer gives a boost to your happy list of I am doing better and my child is happy. That's all you need.

There comes a debate, the baby should come on family food gradually, and the baby should be introduced to the different tastes of family food. This varies from baby to baby as each baby takes their own time to set the eating habits...a mother can add a routine of proper meals and snacks and ensure the gap between the meals. Every house has a different meal timetable, and we set the pattern accordingly.

It is not a cause of worry if the baby throws tantrums while eating, leave the baby and try again. Offer a small portion first, do not intermix the meal time with any other activity like screen time to distract and make them eat while running from here to there. Besides salt and sugar, a disciplined way of eating is most important. That discipline brings ease to our life when we move outside the house, go for vacations, parties, and at any get-together. The environment differs each time, and we cannot provide the same facility when we are in a hurry, and that hinders the baby from enjoying the food as the mind is distracted through a gadget or a toy and not fully enjoying the the food.

Introducing these habits takes time, a month's difficulty, but once you get through this phase, you will undoubtedly feel the difference in your child and other kids. We, as adults, should also practice this discipline as we eat while watching TV. Try to eat together, and eat with your kids whenever possible. The concept of food is quite sacred, and the proper eating habits make it more nutritious. Our entire life goes by earning the bread for our family, and the basic necessity of life is food, and we ignore to make ourselves and our kids accountable for zero wastage of food.

The no salt/sugar drill deviates us from sowing the seeds of the proper eating habits to our kids. It is not a day's work but a gradual process where a mum fails many times, but a mum never gives up. There comes a time when you start introducing self-feeding sessions to the kid. That's another challenge as some kids learn early, and some take time but we compare with others. Every child, even two siblings from the same mum, is not the same; then how can you compare to your neighbours' kid? So, follow your instinct, not as per others' criticisms and nasty comments on your parenting.

Some kids eat well but still seem skinny. Don't you feed them anything? Why are they so thin? Are they malnutrition? Though you know that your kid is eating well, the weight and height are under good progress, you get tired of such remarks and repeat yourself explaining that he/she is absolutely well at each place you visit.

Sometimes not bothering at all is another art of parenting as soon as the kid is active, growing well and pretty active should not be confused with others' opinions...the excellent health of the child matters, their energy levels, and doctor's opinion. Any doubt, consult with the doctor during vaccination visits, check the height and weight from time to time, and if all goes well, stop worrying and start chilling.

Half of the parenting tasks get sorted if we know when to worry and when not to get worried. Unnecessary worries are the main reason that we don't think straight, even in the most manageable situation. For parents, it's mandatory to make the process friendly right from the beginning for the child rather learning these clever tactics of parenthood later in life. These are lifetime skills of balanced parenting as excess of anything doesn't lead us anywhere. Being firm and happy is the demand of today's parenting skills. Witty skills open so many possibilities for comfortable and stress-free parenting...be wise and rise.

Buy Me some 'ME TIME'

What is the most enjoyable thing one would do to experience the importance of... a date with self? We ignore the most important human being in the world while being available for others...others mean others be it anyone. A date with self...a time when you sit with your thoughts, or sometimes nothing at all in mind or heart, its a ME TIME where you want to sit, relax and start the process of exhaling the underlying stress and inhaling the strength to kick the daily dose of even and odds, to be what you are and what you feel. A time when no one defines a woman's role at large, not segregating her into many bits and pieces of responsibilities. Women seek content in small things as they never expected anything more significant than life and never dream of miracles for themselves but others.

She gets lost somewhere at each stage of life... the moment she comes into this world till she departs

from this life. She becomes what others want her to be, how others want to see her, and what others decide for her. If she speaks and becomes upfront, she is not a good woman who is not sacrificing and stating her emotions...that is how we have been raised with a toxic and confined mind set which cages a woman into different boundaries of relationships. We are trying to break the barriers but lack consistency. Sometimes we are full of fire, and sometimes we compromise at our or others' convenience. I, too, matter and there we lack, we underestimate even the petty things we deserve as we have been painted in the image of a sacrificial superwoman. Be a human sometimes and direct life in that direction where you want to see yourself. See life with all the views available from the lens called life. An optimistic view, a cranky view, a neutral perspective, or a view mixed with all the feelings but not losing your own identity while addressing life's adversities. Be fit to lead a lesser complex life as when we are healthy, we can face anything efficiently, but when we need rest, we want to halt at times...please do halt, don't drag yourself unnecessarily. It's always better to reboot yourself like gadgets. We are living beings and if non-living objects need to be updated from time to time, rebooting them makes them work faster, so do not we deserve to reset ourselves...therefore, when the wear and tear of mental and physical strength ask for it, never hesitate.

Money cannot buy everything...a sigh of relief when a mum decides to purchase something exceptionally precious, 'me time' out of their fully-loaded busiest schedule. It is a matter of life choices, a great concern of ensuring the liveliness of that brimming heart, which seeks a positive validation from none other than but herself first.

Me time diaries are dedicated to tiny pleasures of life like pursuing what you like, a long drive, a good read, music, a chit chat, a plate full of delicious delicacies, alone time, or just a cup of tea or coffee in your own space. It's ultimately how you get some time for the renaissance of deep-buried happening hobbies and some of the stuff you never felt like compromising on.

We stop ourselves due to external influences. We are the biggest stumbling block in our own lives and our actions. No separate time will come in the name of when my kids will grow up I will do this or will get time to pursue my dreams. That right time never comes as we have to make it happen gradually, snatching some time from the time available amidst all the responsibilities. Who has seen the very next moment in life in total uncertainty? Go crazy at times, be stubborn, be difficult and see what comes out of that deadly combination of zeal and setting the priorities right.

We can spend ample time on social media peeping into others' life to see what's happening and crib that there's no time but do we ever get down to the real purpose of our own life?

Motherhood itself is a full-time job that requires time management accordingly. We let the external factors set our life goals, hobbies, and aspirations instead of putting our priorities as per the time available.

One has to look beyond the lenses of life and specific responsibilities to frame the ideologies of a balanced, non-cribbing, and blame-game attitude.

Me-time is not about ignoring the responsibilities but taking some time out to do nothing or do what you love to do the most to relax...pampering yourself, grooming, meditation, sleeping, gaming, music, writing, reading, painting, walking, chit-chat, gardening, web series, seeing your neighbours/friends/relatives/parents and list goes on and on...

It is required for unwinding and mental sanity as it is not a waste of time as some women seek me time in small things which bring joy to them for the moment as an achievement that I did something for myself. We often forget to groom ourselves while performing all the duties, we do not recognise the need for mental relaxation. We are just busy running from one hour to another every day. Home-kid-work repeat becomes the sequence, and after a few years, we lose the grip of our creative abilities. We lose interest in many things which used to excite us in life.

Our level of expression, energy, interests, and keen attitude decreases as we grow without modifying our surroundings. Have you ever questioned why we halt during our journeys for a tea and coffee break? To refresh ourselves to break the long tiring drive, to head ahead rejuvenated for another half of the trip. We, as humans, need such refreshment for our interests in the natural riches of life. We become forgetful, endlessly tired in the after-kid journey of parenthood. Parenting is a blissful feeling that becomes tiring as we progress ahead.

We crib but do not do anything to change the situation and carry on with the same mindset, it is not something new as that's what we all have been following from one generation to another. There is an actual need for time-to-time introspection, self-talk, a date with yourself, and a time with your better half where you both can have some time for each other to restore that spark in the relationship. Sometimes these tiny gestures make an immense difference in your situation when you think I am trapped in a vicious circle of responsibilities to manage them happily. Each day is different, and so are we...crib, fight, cry but patch up with your situation and get back to life after every time you lose your temper. Most important is how well you try to know yourself and express yourself accordingly.

Miscommunication is the major flaw in today's relationships, whether with your spouse, children, or friends. We do not convey ourselves correctly and leave things for self-understanding from others. That gets piled up and makes the situation even worst. The skirmish of thoughts and clashes becomes the new normal after the responsibilities are added. We need to create a balance, and over me-time and under me-time will be a matter of worry.

Balance is always required because it paves the way for empathy, humanity, happiness and creativity because happiness and sadness go hand-in-hand... you cannot understand the worth of joy without

 Motherhood Unplugged

been through sorrows and vice-versa. Embrace your challenges, become best buddies with the adversities of your life, widen your horizon and stay optimistic and brave enough to face it all with pure wit and grit...

A Choice : Stroller or Career

The choices that make or break us, define us, or redefine us are essential to get ahead and make a way on which we want to or get forced to walk as there are two choices available always. Some methods are linear, and some are broad enough but require courage to stand firm on the basic principles of how we see life. Staying firm doesn't mean neglecting the family or kids, but I have a life too. We see parenthood as a stumbling block in our society, but kids are not a hindrance, they are an integral part of our lives. How can we say we can not pursue my dreams as I am now a mother. This idea of putting a woman into two chambers of life, either choose this or that right from her early life, has created a vicious circle that she starts seeing herself from others' lenses and never wear her own glasses to see the possibilities, how can I manage if I think of doing something which would satisfy my soul. She wastes her talent all throughout her life that I will do this when my child would go to school, college or job, but that time never comes... We also procrastinate, make excuses, and give ourselves reasons not to advance as we fear annoying others. We always want to see happy faces who are supporting our life choices but agree to disagree is a universal truth that would never be like one thought fit for all. Try to make minor changes, at least one step a day, that is how you'll cross the ocean of hurdles. They are everywhere, but we do not cross when it comes to our lives and choices. We are with everyone in advising, helping, and taking care of, but not with our true selves. We underestimate the power of positive change as either we can make our way or say stagnant regretting later on, the choice is always ours.

A matter of choice, women are always close to the defined spaces of life choices. She thinks she can give away quickly as it's a matter of her baby and the upbringing. Some women do it by choice and some by force as the synchronisation of head and heart doesn't match. Decisions based on people-pleasing, society oriented, neglecting one's own heart is nothing but a sign of great retreat to the individual identity.

Do we ever think my kid should be proud of my life choices rather than creating a vacuum for what I want and do in life? Do we ever try to set an example of our life and the choices we made to do what we like while being equally responsible mothers?

Women are known for their multitasking skills and the epitome of emotions confined in their hearts. We

    Motherhood Unplugged

underestimate ourselves and look down when we have to gear up to absorb life's challenges from a different point of view, with the one size fit for all glasses. We never change the glasses to expand the ambit of our surroundings. Be different, wear the lens of your choice at times, the way you want to see yourself in life qualitatively and quantitatively. I want to see myself as a..........in the next five or ten years. Look around the inspirational women who inspire you. Running a home-based business, writing, painting, cooking, and virtual classes on YouTube makes much more sense than staying stagnant and putting all your energy into meaningless thoughts and cribbing around.

Be the best version of yourself as women are inspiration for the generations to come. If we do something, even if that's the tiniest thing for enhancing ourselves, it becomes an inspiration for others. It works like extending a hand to someone, contributing to life goals.

Therefore, the choice is entirely yours where you need to step out of the comfortable boundaries as one can't move the world while just staying inside the cage of planning and not executing the dreams. Everything comes with a price and you cannot enjoy it as there are no freebies for people who want to create a history despite all their hardships. The highs and lows are the tests of life and should be dealt with passion and high morale as we give up easily. I get tired, I do not get sound sleep, and I do not have family support... support which you should seek is from your partner as there you can expect because both the partners should extend that unconditional helping hand to make things easier for each other.

While pursuing the career, we come back home with the baggage of office work, tensions, and irritation. It always becomes a matter of grave concern, therefore, society demands that women should drop their careers to look after the house and kids to maintain harmony at home. The onus will always be on a mother's shoulder as women are considered to be more emotionally stable and undoubtedly bridge the gap between so many relationships but such a woman fails to manage her career sometimes.

Do not let that happen, as maintaining the zeal with a calm mind and managing skills makes you too different each time you walk that extra mile with your patience. Your immense patience is the key to your success and glory. One has to get through the rings of fire to prove the actual worth of underlying potential. Mark the footsteps of your success, and be a noble and courageous example for your children, as that will always keep you energised towards your life goals to be an all-rounder momma.

A mother is the epitome of excellent knowledge, patience, bravery, love, and happiness. As we say, home is where mum is...a mother makes a home, home...her presence and unconditional love, welcoming the kids when they come back home, her smile makes their day.

The warmth of a mother's love is exceptional as we become a living inspiration for our kids and become passionate about life, which automatically gives a positive signal in the house. kids can relate to your journey, pass it on to their friends, and it will later become bedtime stories to inspire the generation next...

The ambit of parenthood is too vast that you can only reach the different corners of it with your inner light of wisdom and happiness to raise the sun in some dark spaces of so many taboos and myths that hinder a woman's progress when she knows she can manage it all by herself. She requires understanding, support, and faith in her abilities. A fearless environment where she can rely on to re-discover bring her another version other than sister, wife, daughter-in-law, mum, etc.....

A great blend of courage and self-belief is required to start with a thought first that I want to do something...I can manage...I will manage...I am doing it...I did it...

Have never-fading self-esteem to dare the world...

2nd b'day?
2nd baby?

Second Birthday or Second Edition : The terrible twos

Life is running in so many ways as we are busy sustaining better standards of living, competition is high, work pressure is at its peak, handling kids, saving money, vacations, and the list never ends. We do not have time, we do not want it right now, this isn't the right time, we are too busy handling one kid is like a full-time job in itself.

Are we making choices or procrastinating? What do we want? We want to build up a family along with kids as they need a guarantee in life after us in the name of their DNA. We never take a tough call before extending our family, whether ready or not. Sometimes it's like we have a baby girl, so we need a baby boy to complete our family. This word 'complete' confuses me. Aren't we complete if we do not want to have another baby? Is that child deprived of fundamental human rights if they do not have a sibling? Do we worry about our child's happiness or the time we can give to our kids? We are fulfilling their needs, putting them in certain activities, making them competitive, but that parental time to feel complete without any biases, without that calculation in mind, one or two kids. Have kids as much as one wants, but we should not comprehend it in the way of task completion.

Family is not a task completion if one opts for one or three babies. We are never satisfied, even in terms of our offspring. We are constantly doing things according to societal norms but not what we want from life, what we feel like a family. What is our bond with one another? Then we see kids as a matter of responsibility, when our life is stuck, that is our choice, and we are never delighted after making that choice. We need to redefine the goal of our life when we see ourselves as parents as whatever may be the case, humans should be happy first instead of completing the tasks. Some parents are more satisfied with one kid only, some are most happy without kids, and some are balancing lives with three kids as well. It is all about how we respond to what we choose...our choices define us.

The phase of planning, thinking, and much more hovers over the parents' heads. Meanwhile, parents cross so many milestones along with the child to reach at the very first happy birthday that there's a constant reminder whistling around...what about the second one? Once the first birthday phase is over, the naughtiest and craziest stages begin to turn the entire schedule upside down. Parents usually struggle to channelise such an intense energy level of the toddler, and the physical and psychological reminders are another addition to the decision making.

This decision-making cannot only be emotions centric, or a sibling centric. We must expand the arenas of thinking thoughtfully, a blend of practicality backed by emotional sense.

Don't be in a hurry, every parent's choice is different... sometimes the finances restrict, sometimes the marital issues, you are not ready, maybe you will be prepared afterward, sometimes it's the time constraints, and sometimes you are more than satisfied having one child to complete your family.

Do follow your heart and what suits you best in your circumstances. People around us are there to share their viewpoint on this much-discussed topic, but we will have to war-game between wants and needs as there is quite a thin line between them.

Your happiness and the bond between husband and wife as a team matter. The goal should be to stay happy, divide, and understand the gist of responsibilities, as parenting is a never-ending task. The environment of the house should be positive and welcome the new life with grace rather than merely a burden at the back of your mind.

The terrible 2s are the initial years of the upbringing of the child, where matching with his/her super energy becomes a task and dealing with two kids at the same time makes you a perfect referee...jokes apart, the future phases where the development of the child is on peak and when they start understanding and noticing their environment one has to be cautious enough for being positive and the arguments at home should be dealt privately.

Kids understand, but they cannot be made understand with explanations about certain things. They register some of the bad events of childhood back in their mind lifelong, so we must try to avoid such situations in all the ways possible. The terrible 2s should always be remembered as happy memories for the parents and kids, not in a terrible sense.

One should settle down the routine and academic life of the first one. A mum should spend a lot of time recovering entirely from the first pregnancy, shed the last leftover pregnancy weight, consult a doctor and then conclude by fixing the minor loopholes of constraints and assets how much your mind and body are in sync to get ahead to have another baby.

The time has changed, nuclear family system has replaced the joint family culture, job constraints, more issues if both the parents are working, and leaving the kid at the daycare centre, is the new normal. Balancing is an art along with life and parenthood needs a proper assessment. We need to be wise enough to cater the well-being of two kids in its entirety. A child should have a companion and sibling to get along with in life, but certain things cannot be neglected, and the decision should not be made in haste and entirely based on others' opinions.

Constructive opinions are always welcomed when you hear from your actual well-wishers. Do seek opinions, go through all the even and odds of this planning, and be honest with yourself and your circumstances as one cannot conclude it in the air. Constructive and well-thought-through planning is required to see the possibilities. Many of us plan because our baby needs a sibling. There are many other aspects of having sibling as kids learn to share, learn to co-operate, and provide a support system for the future, but all we look into the linear side of it, we need to complete a family, and they need a sibling. Because many parents do not believe in it and meet their family with one kid, it doesn't mean their family is incomplete.

Therefore, it should be one's choice to decide as it should come from the heart. It would help if you are keen and enthusiastic about bringing another life into this world. That excitement makes this parenting a more blissful journey than a tiring one and a positive example for our fellow parents, and we all need to have better family planning talks as it is much required in our country.

Pre School Tantrums

Tantrums are the new normal for parents when handling kids. It's difficult for parents and kids to leave behind an era of their comfort zone and step into a new horizon of different people. That tests the patience from both sides as the learning takes place. We often complain but never figure out the psychology behind a child's new vulnerabilities. An average human would show all the signs of anxiety, happiness, excitement, sadness, and associated emotions. So, the child is also a human offspring and has the right to portray human emotions. When there is encouragement, the child feels motivated and starts doing well, which is a healthy progress. One step at a time, but we sometimes overburden the kid, making them learn multiple activities, which confuses the child and causes a lack of concentration. We sometimes become too competitive that we forget the basics of learning. Learning means happy learning how much a child can handle or enjoy doing, be it anything. When we force or impose, that creates a rift in the proper upbringing of a child. Get along with the child; do not run ahead or chase kids, be a part of that journey, that learning, that fun and stress-busting joys of early childhood moments.

From one phase to another, potty training to school orientation, finding the best, competition among the friends, and the list goes on and on... Many things cause many worries in parents' minds. How will the kid manage? How are we going to concentrate on work in those few hours when the child is away? There is a constant tick-tick in mind.

We, as parents, tend to get over-protected and seek comfort for our kids everywhere, which is normal. We want our kids to be independent, outspoken and excelling in life right from the beginning.

It is a crucial phase for the kids who will be stepping out to interact with their new friends, where the child would be fed by the caretaker of the pre-school or sometimes by the teacher. But there will be no mum, no dad to supervise. The kid gets irritated initially as he/she would cry inconsolably as they are also leaving their comfort zone, therefore, a few days to weeks tantrums are absolutely norma...but after some time, the kid starts enjoying that routine of friends, activities, and fun at pre-school which paves the way for the formal schooling.

Many parents think of intermixing this learn with fun time with rigorous academic learning, and then the chain of endless comparison and competition starts. This time is dedicated for adapting to the new environment of fun and games, every kid is different. Some like to write, some like to draw, some like to paint, or some are just there to eat and have fun. As parents, your achievement is not defined in the context of how many alphabets your ward knows to read and write, instead, is he/she happy, getting disciplined to a minor extent, enjoying interacting with friends, started eating on his/her own or not...

Life's significant lessons originate from essential grass-root level learnings. Academics and manners goes hand-in-hand, one without another os futile. There is humongous competition everywhere, but do not prevent your kid from enjoying what they deserve at this age in terms of happiness, give more weightage to happiness over other things. We set standards from the beginning, and that's how we do not promote excellence and run after intellect, instead, percentages, trophies etc...There must be a balance between your expectations from the child and his/her capacity.

Kids do not understand what they want to become, and there comes this confusion about what to do in life. Imposed choices are the biggest hindrance in the way of creative generations. How many of us seek excellence in life? Don't we live our lives as per others' viewpoints mostly? Don't we want our kids to pursue what others are pursuing than looking after the things which interest them...We all hardly bother.

Parenting is not an isolated process but a mixture

of raising responsible, creative, and great decision-makers...our generations should be responsible citizens and an asset to the society. We should see parenting as an integral part for doing something great for the nation by raising high-class citizens.

Don't go with the herd who believes in setting a trend of parenting, career choices, fashion, and so on...be the kind of parents you want to be as per your instinct and inculcate that habit in your kids right from the beginning. Proper decision-making is an art that is an essential skill we all should have as our brain is a precious gift from God. We do not believe in our innate abilities and dilute our God-gifted powers in the influence of others. We quickly get influenced by every good and bad thing around us. That's why mid-way and the art of balancing to get along with our surroundings is an ongoing everlasting task that tests our patience. The kind of decisions we make define our hidden abilities to be different, to do something different to create a history.

Ambitiously Guilty

Ambitions...a woman can never have them peacefully as she is always in a dilemma or self-doubts. She never recovers from that guilt of pursuing her dreams, leaving the baby for a couple of hours, or if she goes out with her friends to have some time to reboot herself. She goes hurriedly and comes back even more hurriedly. That hurry in which she is trying to fill herself in all the spaces of life and that constant worry divides her as she never enjoys herself thoroughly wherever she is. A continuous clock of her time is tickling from one place to another. Sometimes it's good not to think beyond our mental capacity. Women think beyond when they know the reality and the coarse of their lives. All-time dying a little, not meeting the requirements, and missing some events are part of life as mothers cannot be omnipresent at every hour. We over pamper people around us that they start staying over-dependent on us.

When we feel the burden, we crib like all humans do but still carry forward with that guilt endlessly. We expect too much from our capacities to handle. That is why we are primarily unhappy out of assuming life most of the time. Sometimes it's good to leave things and situations on their own, what it means to see a well-intact home of a working mother if you have never seen a messy house or kitchen on her to-do list for the weekend. Pending laundry to the homework of kids is an experience of its kind when you meet the deadlines on your toes. How much you enjoy doing all of this and how much you are dragging yourself matters. The roller coaster ride of life is to enjoy sometimes, sometimes, you can take an off from home but never stop believing in yourself and the dreams you carry in your head and heart.

Women are raised with a mindset to fulfil all the expectations in each phase of their lives...a never-ending journey from birth to death. She has multiple roles to play, and majorly her contribution counts as a mother who has raised her kids, whether she is a homemaker or a working mum.

There are multiple successful women examples, making it easier for other women to dream about their ambitions. It varies from woman to woman as some gave up everything to look after the child, some don't want to, but their circumstances force them to pursue and then another category of women who dare to dream of managing as they challenge the adversities of life, they desire to own feed their soul and yet fulfil all the motherly responsibilities along.

There are pros and cons of everything...working mums do not get much time to spend, sometimes work pressure and sometimes the body's capacity gives up. Dreams ask for a price at each level in life...the price is that you will have to miss something somewhere, you cannot be present everywhere, and sometimes prioritising between work, home and kids nudge a woman to such an extent that after-effects are full of being in a guilty state of mind.

Easy! It's with everyone, even the fathers comes in the same category as they are always at the receiving end. A father's contribution is always underrated in the field of parenting. We, as a society counts the sacrifices of a mother but never look at the fathers that they miss those moments when they also feel like being present for the kid the family most of the time.

The hustle and bustle of life will never be at ease as we live in a world of aspirations, ambitions, and competition...why do we do all this? It is all for raising a child in a better, more secure environment.

We, sometimes seek validation from others and forget the essence of staying happy the way we are. We failed to behave like normal humans that it wasn't my day. As parents, we should always aspire to be satisfied whether we are busy or busiest and make the most of the spare time when home to unwind on a happy note instead of feeling guilty for no reason.

Our ambitions and the zeal to do something in life make us alive. We forget to maintain the mental sanity with the most critical person in our life, and that is our own real self...a true self who wants to do something like becoming a parent is not a crime that one should feel like they are jailed or in a cage of never-ending responsibilities...that is a part of our life which should go along with our dreams which we have seen for ourselves as parenting is not a hindrance instead we are slaves of our negativity and seeking comfort zones time to time. You cannot cross the sea by mere standing at the shore.

We think we will win all the battles of life without facing the battlefield. We do not want to be courageous enough to break the prejudices and even if we do then embrace our hearts with a lot of self-guilt without realising that you have different responsibilities and giving your best as per your situation is the only way to make peace with life, parenting, home, and work.

We do not want to face the criticisms, but can you make a diamond shine without rubbing it rigorously?

Motherhood Unplugged

James Bond of the House

Women are equal but different. They are an epitome of hope, belief, and a link between many relationships. She has always emerged as a building block for sustaining and maintaining relationships with all the individuals around her. She is a go-to person, a friend, a companion, a soulmate, and a strong woman who is an entire world on her own. She is someone who is an emerging star in every place she belongs and denotes to. She embraces the negatives with courage and a never-tiring attitude, making her a goddess of life as God has given her all the ingredients and she collected all of them to make beautiful relationships from them, from being kitchen queen to the boss lady at work. This superwoman plays all the roles parallel and is a manager of all the lives surrounding herself. The transformation of a woman from her adolescent to a young woman teaches her the art of being patient enough with life. The cycle of her life turns many tides of positive and negative impacts, and that's how a woman becomes stronger and wise. Those experiences become her guides that she counsel others from her own experiences in life, and people start relating themselves. Encouragement and motivation become easy for others as she makes life easier for her partner, friends, colleagues, boss, and kids. Even the indulgence in non-living things also becomes lively in her cheerful presence. A woman who goes through all this while performing her duties can be nasty and demanding also at times, so can't we handle her at her worst as all she needs is a shoulder to rest, to feel important, to feel heard and held when she is on the verge of giving up on things as if some days she shines then there are the days when it rains in her life too like all the seasons, life of every individual also goes through the happy-sad-content-neutral phases of life.

A woman is an entire world to the child, and the people live in that house. Home-maker home creator, home is where mom is...so many responsibilities and much more expectations to fulfil throughout her life span...

Her aura is a magical motivation to raise each being around her...raising a child to create a particular arcade to cater to the needs of the house as per demand...on the toes is the word.

Mother's Day and Women's Day are the days that are celebrated throughout the world to acknowledge her significance in life, I agree with the idea behind these celebrations as women never recognise their contributions, therefore, a day especially meant to make themselves aware that how special they are, they owe a toast to themselves as a matter of the fact that they are doing better in whatever field they are, be it office, home, pursuing a wonderful hobby, single, married, divorced, a mother or not a mother...she doesn't need a tag to define her courage and the acts of daily life...

A woman is a collective word in itself as she is a nucleus of qualities like determination, compassion, patience, zeal, and a never-fading selfless outlook towards life to look ahead in all the ups and downs of life.

Her opinionated mind makes her different, to make a new way to change the coarse of her destiny at times. Certain taboos cannot hold her back from achieving the riches of internal faith and a fighter's attitude. Her competition each day is with her old age insecurities imbibed in her in the name of perfect 'sanskars' and meaningless compromises. A woman has re-oriented her entire system of critical thinking to understand the concept of actual feminism in the 21st century,

She walked many miles to avoid her typical easy choices to re-write the history. Many thanks to those women in history and those who dared to dream to form a distinctive chain of hope and aspirations.

Does it all come quickly? Not at all. One has to pay the price for making dreams a reality, making them work as the challenges are different, but the vibe cannot be differentiated. Women are known for their God-gifted ability to handle things well mentally and emotionally. Empathy is naturally available among women but half of the life we spend doubting our abilities.

You are an epitome of immense hard work, handling pressure, and relationships, carrying yourself with a smile of hope for others in all the highs and lows of life. The tactics of parenthood to handle the childhood tantrums to adolescent counselling, later on becoming friends with the young lad...

Life unfolds so that we keep progressing with time and perform our duties as per their needs and demands. Demands of time and demands from our aspirations somewhere in the heart keep that hope alive and delist all the hardships and odds of this journey. After the thirties, life changes, some physical changes, hormonal changes, weight gain, weight loss, and career are at the peak of all joys and pressures as growth in trade brings responsibilities along.

One who knows the art of recognising their core strength and weaknesses can win over after failing each time, from making the worst decisions to speaking as the wisest person on this earth, as experiences enhance us each time we grow if we learn from them constructively and positively. Therefore, a lot is required to achieve the title of a superwoman.

Women do not work to achieve tags but selflessly, which makes them different from others as they earn respect with their unconditional service to all the relations around them...they knot these pearls in a string of hope, courage, patience, and determination. They become an ideal example of the purest form of love on this earth where no one can ever match that love.

Parenting : A Modern Outlook

There are many versions of parenthood in which some events of our kids teach us and we learn and un-learn from them, and kids imitate our actions and also choose to learn and un-learn from their parents. In the entire journey, each day is quantitative and qualitative. We do not want to war-game between the two as what are the issues of actual concern and what are we focusing on is something to look into. The balance between the two is the actual art of healthy parenting. There is no category like perfect parenting, but happy parenting and happy raising should be the focus areas. In the modern world of many possibilities and comforts, we have lost the essence of being humans. As we want to substitute everything with gadgets and activities but sometimes doing nothing, staying with the child organically without distracting ourselves makes much sense. It sows the seeds of mindfulness for both parents and kids. We pay a lot of money to learn mindfulness and stay joyful but never give importance to little self-made efforts in our lives.

We want someone else to do what we are required to do. Little efforts with consistency make a visible difference. We are too busy out of nothing at times that we have conditioned ourselves to go with that artificial flow. To make them learn art, we do not have to be MF Hussain, but an abstract way of simply carving out the artistic mind in a child doesn't require any tutor at initial levels, which needs a parental bond other than a professional coach. The same goes for other activities, such as cooking, reading, colouring, writing, or learning. Learning is a natural process, we should instil innate abilities in ourselves and our kids. We also re-discover our hidden skills of being patient, communicators, discipline, and most importantly...digital detox as humans can discover and innovate many other skills if they direct them positively and consistently to revolutionise the world of parenting. With the help of technology-driven parenting, we have become stagnant that our creative mind is always busy googling somewhere.

We want to be super parents, perfect parents but we do not want to excel in the fields of happiness as my central message to all the parents is to stay happy first rest will follow. You will achieve all the milestones which you would set for yourself. Staying happy is the first key to unlocking the levels of parenting.

Parenting is indeed a challenging job, it's not gender-centric but somewhat difficult for both the partners. Being a parent is a team work, not an individual task, and it becomes challenging.

In a modern world, our lives are much more occupied with work, home, and maintaining an excellent social life schedule. They are just part of life and occupy a reasonable amount of time even if it's only restricted to social media...taking endless pictures in the house, outside the home, video calls, clicking before you eat, flaunting the family trips, WhatsApping in the broadcast list of your contacts and the list goes on and on...

It's not anyone's fault as these things are the new normal. Due to COVID, these have become an absolute part of our lives as everything is just a click away. In this entire routine, we never quantify the time we have given to our parents, spouse, and children...sitting in the same room but keeping a child busy in some activity to surf for an extra hour, to see what people are doing, wearing, partying about as we are so much into knowing others lifestyle, we never introspect how did we spend our day in a constructive or futile way. We are getting distant from ourselves leave others.

Modern parenting is quite a techie thing, but the essence of warmth in relationships is getting compromised. We must look into how much time we smile for ourselves and not just for the sake of a good selfie or to showcase a happy family frame. We are getting ahead of time, becoming more social and more available to the world that sometimes we have to make those blue ticks dysfunctional to prioritise our own life at times.

What are we passing on to the next generation?

They replicate what they see. Kids eat their food while the rhymes are on. While making our lives easier, we are imbibing a different kind of vicious circle around our kids. We are deviating them from some divine feelings and experiences exist in the world like reading a book, having a chit-chat session during meals, family bonding, family activities, a day dedicated as 'no gadget day'...finding pleasure in nature, and connecting ourselves to the idea of a having an actual life.

We, as parents, are not passing on the kind of childhood we enjoyed but instead regressing ourselves in this techie world of gadgets. We should get ahead with time, but a mid-path is always a solution to be different in such a modern world.

With the technology and how artificial intelligence is progressing rapidly, we will see a remarkable change shortly. Still, as I consistently stressed on creating a balance as per your convenience would be a significant achievement because we no longer use our creative intellect because everything is readily available. Online learning has impacted hugely on the interpersonal skills of children. Working professionals have forgotten about the get-along attitude with others as that leads to a poor tolerance level and miscommunication adds on another burden in complicating our lives as we have become unable to express ourselves in words as emoticons have become another new normal where we compliment either with emojis or stickers.

We are inculcating a habit of shortcuts and a laid-back attitude in this technologically advanced world

Motherhood Unplugged

of gadgets and gimmicks. What we do, our kids learn the same mindset, and we cannot correct them by not mending our ways first. Parenting is a lifelong journey where you learn and unlearn many things, sometimes, we learn from our kids, and they teach us to be better than our previous version. It goes hand-in-hand; it's both ways, and exchanging ideas givesit a holistic approach. To make it more collective, we must learn to unlearn bad practices that have become integral to our routine. The unaccountability of time is a grave concern, but we don't realise it, and by following this routine, we become slaves to our bad habits. To end this slavery of laid-back attitude and non-disciplined approach must be brought to an accountable outlook to work on it gradually as a whole team we call a family.

I would conclude by quoting one of the aptest excerpts from our Father of the nation, which was written back in time but still makes an absolute sense to direct our wisdom towards raising India Class citizens.

"Children inherit the parents' qualities, no less than their physical features. The environment does play an important part, but the original capital on which a child starts in life is inherited from its ancestors. I have also seen children successfully surmounting the effects of an evil inherence. That is due to purity being an inherent attribute of the soul".

Mahatma Gandhi (1948). "Autobiography: The Story of Experiments with Truth," p. 276, Courier Corporation.

Epilogue

The challenges of motherhood are never really ending but what actually needs to end is the imbibed art of procrastination. No one is perfect and that's the real life which made me learn and unlearn many times. From a naive mother-to-be to a mum who is not so perfect, I have walked many miles ahead. My son made me learn a lot of things that I never imagned I would ever learn in life, patience is the major learning among them. My journey to start writing a book was not at all a cake walk because when women think of doing something in life, they need to cross a ring of so many responsibilities. I never thought that I would be able to manage, tried–failed–tried...this is a process one has to go through. I procrastinated a lot, self doubts, mood swings, recovering post pregnancy and tons of responsibilities. I warned myself that before I start losing my own ability to do something, better buck up and try to manage. A self talk with your own self is the most important regimen one should start practicing. We women never get time to talk to our inner self patiently. I corrected myself gradually as it's not an overnight process to unlearn the bad practices and to inculcate new habis to re-discover yourself.

Some of my chapters are repetitive, they are so because we need to push to break the shackles of our laid back attitude. It is with all of us, even though I had been through the same but as I inisteed self-talk is the key. Women are everything, a daughter, a wife, a sister, a mum and so on but they are not humans...they have been considered goddesses but why do we need to be a goddess? Goddesses become idols, are we really a statue of sacrifice and tolerance? Why women just cannot be just humans who feel, who express and speak when it's needed...I have faced so many hardships to find some of the answers for my mental sanity. I can be a good mum when I am sorted in my own life. We tend to live a dual life, a life which others want us to live, and a life which we have in our subconscious memory, the way we are supposed to live. Our aspirations and expectations will always vary but our efforts should bridge this difference. I burned many bridges to create new bridges of positivity, strength and happiness. We cannot be dependent upon others to be happy as women are the creators of life on this earth but live quietly a deprived life. My only message to all my readers is that one step at a time and a consistent effort would create a huge difference in your life. Please do live for yourself as well. Children are the building block of our life, not the stumbling block. Emotions and practicality of life are two different roads

which go along with a balance and we are supposed
to educate our offspring about the true values of this
human life, as this life is for a noble purpose and most
of it gets wasted living it superficially. Please create a
balance between your head and heart as it's an art and
women are blessed with Emotional Quotient and that's
what makes them equal but different.